characters created by lauren child

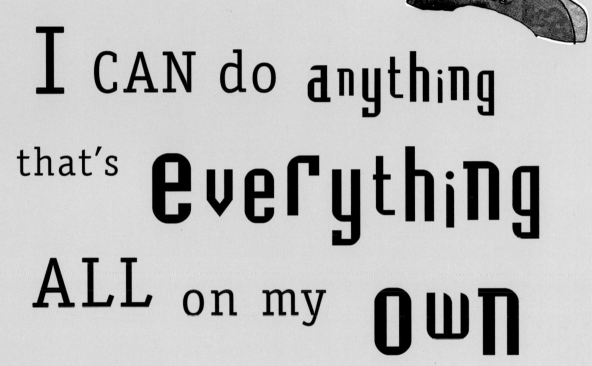

I CAN do anything that's everything ALL on my own

PUFFIN

Text based on the script written by
Carol Noble & Bridget Hurst

Illustrations from the TV animation

produced by Tiger Aspect

PUFFIN BOOKS
Published by the Penguin Group: London, New York, Australia,
Canada, India, Ireland, New Zealand and South Africa
Penguin Books Ltd, Registered Offices: 80 Strand, London WC2R 0RL, England

puffinbooks.com

This edition published in Great Britain in Puffin Books 2010
1 3 5 7 9 8 6 4 2
Text and illustrations copyright © Lauren Child / Tiger Aspect Productions Limited, 2008
The Charlie and Lola Logo is a trademark of Lauren Child
All rights reserved. The moral right of the author/illustrator has been asserted
Manufactured in China
ISBN: 978-0-141-33491-2
This edition produced for The Book People Ltd,
Hall Wood Avenue, Haydock, St Helens, WA11 9UL

I have this little sister Lola.
She is small and very funny.
At the moment, Lola likes to say,
"I can do **anything** that's **everything**
ALL on my **own**."

Lola says,
"I can button up my coat
ALL on my own.

I can use the computer
ALL on my own.

And I can DEFINITELY
pour pink milk
ALL on my own."

I say, "Let me **help**, Lola."

But she says, "**NO.**
I can do **anything**
        that's **everything**
ALL on my **own**."

So then I say,
    "Lola, **helping** is
VERY important.

    What about the
milk monkeys
        in the jungle?

How do you think
        they get their
pink milk?

"They HELP each other!

If the **monkeys**
tried to do this
            ALL on their **own**,
they would
NEVER get their
            pink milk."

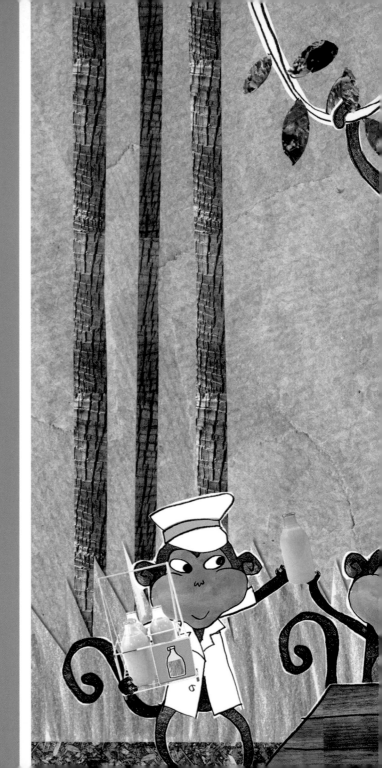

"But I am NOT
            a monkey
so I do not need
            any help,"
says Lola.

"I can do anything
that's everything
      ALL on my own."

Later,
Marv and Lola and me
go to the park.

Marv says,
"Lola, do you want
to play piggy
in the middle?"

And Lola says,
"NO thank you.

I am going to
the playground to swing
ALL on my own."

Then I say,
"Hey, Lola. Do you want
to play with us?"

She says,
"NO thank you, Charlie.

Next I will be playing
on the see-saw
ALL on my own."

Then Marv says,
    "But the see-saw
will not SEE or SAW
    with only one person."

And I say, "Yes.
    You need two people
to go up in the air."

But Lola says,
    "Why would I want
to go high up
        when I can see
LOTS of interesting things
    very close and near
to the ground?"

So I say, "But Lola,
　　　being high up
can be REALLY fantastic."

Then Marv and me
　　　get on the see-saw
and Lola goes high up
　　　in the air.

I say, "What can you see,
　　　Captain Lola?"

"I can see a
GIANT octopus," says Lola,
"And I can see...

"...PIRATES!
And they are coming
to get us!"

We shout, "HELP!
Captain Lola! HELP!"

"Don't worry, Charlie!
Don't worry, Marv!
I will **rescue** you."

Then Lola says,
"See, Charlie?
        I saved you
AND Marv from the
EVER-so-mean pirates.

You couldn't
untie yourselves
        on your own,
could you?

I can do anything
        that's everything
ALL on my own!"

And I say, "Yes, Lola. You CAN do everything
all on your own... except WALK home."
     And do you know what Lola says then?
"Oh, Charlie, walking home isn't any fun
                    ALL on my own."